# Strictly Come Dancing

# ROCK 'n' ROLLING

*"So much fun – especially the dancing bits!"*
Janine, 7

★

*"The book was thrilling, exciting,*
*magical and happy."*
Elise, 10

★

*"It was a very happy story and I wanted to get to*
*the next chapter to see what would happen next."*
Lucy, 6

★

*"A great book."*
Evie, 8

★

*"I thought it was good ... I like the drawings."*

A Catalogue record for this book is available from
the British Library

ISBN: 978 1 444 90966 1

Printed and bound by CPI Group
(UK) Ltd, Croydon, CR0 4YY

The paper and board used in this paperback by Hodder Children's
Books are natural recyclable products made from wood grown in
sustainable forests. The manufacturing processes conform to the
environmental regulations of the country of origin.

Hodder Children's Books
a division of Hachette Children's Books
338 Euston Road, London NW1 3BH
An Hachette UK company
www.hachette.co.uk

# ROCK 'n' ROLLING

## Chloe Melody

Hodder
Children's
Books

A division of Hachette Children's Books

★ *Meet the Professional Dancers from* ★

Strictly Come Dancing

Kristina Rihanoff

★ **Which three words best describe the rock 'n' roll to you?**

Fun, speed and power!

★ **How old were you when you discovered you loved to dance?**

I have danced for as long as I can remember but I was probably about six when I decided I want to dance for the rest of my life!

★ **Did you go to a special dance academy like Bella?**

Yes, at the age of six I was invited to a ballroom dance school.

★ **How old were you when you won your first dance competition?**

I was seven and my partner and I were so excited! We had no fear as we just wanted to dance. Our enjoyment must have come through as we won! It was a small local competition but it felt so important to us.

★ **What is your favourite dance and why?**

My favourite dance is the rumba. It is the slowest of all Latin dances. The music is really beautiful and you can do a lot of amazing tricks and show off your flexibility.

**Turn the page to find out how Bella learns to dance the rock 'n' roll ...**

Humming to herself, Bella Jones
finished brushing her hair and put on
her lucky sparkly heart-shaped earrings.
She usually only wore these on special
occasions, but she had a feeling that
today might just turn out to be one of
them.

Mind you, she thought, smiling at
her reflection and smoothing down a
stray strand of hair, ever since she'd

auditioned and earned herself a place at the Strictly Dance Academy, *every* day had become special. Bella still couldn't quite believe that she was now living and training at the famous London dance school, and was loving every minute. Talk about a dream come true!

"Aaargh!" cried out a cross voice just then. Bella turned in surprise, only to see a tap shoe whizz through the air. Natalie, one of her roommates, was peering into her wardrobe, throwing out clothes, shoes and everything else as she searched for something. "Where *are* they?" she wailed.

"What are you looking for?" Bella asked. She had met Natalie at their first audition for the academy and liked her immediately. Natalie was American, and a real livewire – fun, bouncy and energetic. She didn't seem very happy today though.

"I can't find my favourite ballet shoes," she grumbled, running a hand through her tight dark curls. "You haven't seen them, have you? I've hunted everywhere!"

"No," Bella replied, "but I'll help you look."

"Me too," offered Sofia, who also shared the room. She was half-Italian and had gorgeous long black hair and olive skin. As well as being kind and loyal, she was also a brilliant dancer, and the three girls had really hit it off since joining the academy. Recently, they'd all been lucky enough to get picked to dance with the famous boy band New Ride at a carnival too. Now *that* was something none of them would forget in a hurry!

With a graceful leap from her bed, Sofia joined Bella and Natalie by the wardrobe which was rapidly becoming empty. "They've got to be here *somewhere*," Natalie said, tossing a pink leotard over her shoulder.

"Looking for these, by any chance?" a smug voice called out. Bella, Natalie and Sofia swung round to see Veronica, the fourth member of their dorm, in the doorway. She walked in, gingerly holding a pair of ballet shoes by the tips of her fingers as if worried she might catch something from them.

Natalie leapt to her feet. "My shoes! Thanks, dude! Where did you find them?"

Veronica looked horrified to be called

* * * 5 * * *

"dude". She was blonde, pretty and a major snob. "I must have picked them up by mistake," she replied coolly. "They're far too big for me, of course. What gigantic feet you have, Natalie!"

Bella winced, wishing Veronica wouldn't always be so mean. She wasn't convinced Veronica had picked up the shoes by mistake either. It would be just like her to take them on purpose, knowing it would send Natalie into a panic.

Natalie wasn't the sort of person you could push around though. She snatched her shoes and glared back defiantly. "So what does that make you, Princess Dainty-toes?" she scoffed. She pointed at her name which had been written inside each shoe. "See? Next time CHECK!"

Uh-oh. Now Veronica looked positively murderous. "Guys," Bella said quickly, trying to smooth things over. "Let's just calm down a bit ..."

But Veronica was in no mood to calm down. "Don't you *dare* speak to me like that!" she hissed at Natalie, her eyes blazing. "Or I'll—"

Thankfully, before they could find out exactly *what* Veronica was about to threaten, the door opened and in came Emma, their fifteen-year-old dorm monitor, and a dance star in the making. Veronica fell silent and tossed her hair crossly while Natalie bent down to put away her scattered belongings, still scowling.

Emma raised her eyebrows. "Is

everything all right in here?" she asked.
"I thought I heard an argument ..."

"Everything's fine," Bella said hastily.

"Just talking," Sofia added, jumping to
her feet.

"Good," Emma replied, although
she didn't look convinced. "I came to
give you some news anyway. There's a
special meeting after lunch today, before
dance practice."

"What sort of special meeting?" asked
Bella, her ears pricking up with interest.

Emma smiled. "That's the big
mystery," she replied. "Nobody knows.
You'll just have to wait to find out, I'm
afraid." She glanced up at the clock.
"I'll see you later. Lessons start in ten
minutes, so make sure you're ready."

Natalie collapsed dramatically on to her bed once Emma had left the room. "We have to wait all morning to find out the big exciting secret? Noooo!"

Everyone laughed – apart from Veronica. "Hopefully it's a meeting to announce that they've decided to turf out the amateur dancers," she muttered under her breath. And with that, she swept out of the room, her nose in the air.

Bella flushed. Veronica was always making snide remarks about "amateur" dancers, just because Bella had never had any formal dance training before coming to the academy, unlike the others.

"Ignore her," Sofia said loyally, just

as Natalie sang out "JEALOUS!" after Veronica's departing footsteps.

Bella felt grateful for her friends' support.

What would she do without them?

**2**

The morning seemed to drag horribly slowly as the students sat through maths and science. At the academy there were always ordinary school lessons until lunchtime followed by dance classes all afternoon.

As Bella and her friends ate lunch, she noticed a definite feeling of excitement in the air. Everyone was talking about what the "special meeting" might

be about. Some of the boys, Jason
and Mark, were convinced that they
would get to appear on Strictly Come
Dancing. A group of girls who'd been
disappointed not to take part in the
carnival with New Ride were hopefully
discussing which other pop groups
they'd like to dance with. Bella, Natalie
and Sofia, meanwhile, wondered if they
might be taken to see a famous ballet, or
West End show as a treat.

At last, lunch was over and Bella and
her roommates changed into their
dance gear. They'd been told to wear
their jazz shoes for the first lesson today,
and Bella made sure her laces were tied
tightly. Her jazz shoes were made of soft
black leather with a small heel, and a

rubber sole. They barely made a
sound as she hurried down to
the practice studio, a
fluttery feeling starting
up in her tummy. She
couldn't wait to find
out the big secret!

Miss Anna, their teacher, walked in
and the studio fell silent. It seemed as if
everyone was holding their breath with
excitement, Bella thought.

"Good afternoon, children," Miss Anna
said. She was originally from Russia
and spoke with a strong accent. "I'm
delighted to bring you some th*rrrrr*illing
news. Today you will be dancing for
the world-famous theatre director, Mr
Manuel Diago. He's looking for dancers

to take part in a special gala show."

A gasp of excitement went around the studio. "No *way*," breathed Sofia, her dark eyes shining.

"Bring it on!" Natalie cheered, high-fiving Sofia and Bella.

"I can't believe it," Bella said, feeling tingly all over. Hadn't she known today was going to turn out special? You didn't get much more special than dancing for a world-famous theatre director ... and auditioning for his show!

Just then, Mr Diago himself walked in, and everybody gasped again. Even

super-cool Veronica looked pink in
the cheeks and clutched at one of

her friends.

*Wow*, thought
Bella, watching
as he went to
join Miss Anna.
Manuel Diago had
written and directed
lots of famous West
End musicals ... and
here he was right now,
standing in front of
them. She couldn't

wait to phone her mum and dad later
and tell them. Life at the Strictly Dance
Academy just got more extraordinary by
the day!

"Hello everyone," said Mr Diago, smiling around the room. "I'm here today because I'm putting on a special gala performance of my musical, Slick, and I'm looking for three couples to perform a rock 'n' roll routine as part of the show. Have any of you done any rock 'n' roll dancing before?"

A few people put up their hands, but Bella kept hers still. She'd never done *any* formal dance classes before coming to the academy, and wasn't even quite sure what rock 'n' roll dancing was.

Veronica proudly held her hand up high and shot Bella a triumphant look as she did so. Bella blushed. No doubt Veronica was thinking what an amateur she was again.

Miss Anna's blue eyes twinkled. "Rock 'n' roll dancing is great fun," she told them. "But it is very athletic and hard work. It originated from a type of dance called the lindy hop, and is  performed in couples or groups."

"There are lots of kicks, jumps, throws and flips in rock 'n' roll dancing," Mr Diago continued, then grinned. "In fact, I've brought along a few friends to show you how it's done. Guys!" he called. "When you're ready, please!" He flicked on some music and a bouncy tune began. Bella found herself tapping her feet to the rhythm … and then in rushed Matt and Velma, two of the professional dancers from Strictly Come Dancing, wearing bright costumes and funky shoes. Matt wore a loud red shirt with big collars and pointed shoes, and had his hair gelled forward into a quiff. Velma wore a dress which was fitted on top with an enormous skirt and lots of petticoats underneath.

"Wow," Bella breathed to herself. The famous dancers used the dance studios at the academy for rehearsals – but Bella

still got a thrill when she saw them in
real life.

They began by facing each other and
holding hands, then
stepping towards
one another
and back
with small
kicks from
the knee. *So far,
so straightforward,*
thought Bella – but
then the man
grabbed his partner
and lifted her so that
she went right over
his head and on to
his back. Without

missing a beat, he reached through his legs and smoothly pulled her all the way through, so that she was facing him once again. All of this happened in the blink of an eye.

"Mamma mia," Sofia murmured, looking impressed.

And so the dance went on, with lots of spins, kicks and energy. Bella's feet twitched. She couldn't wait to start learning some of the moves for herself!

Everyone clapped as the routine ended, and the dancers bowed, grinning, before leaving the studio once more. "Don't worry," Mr Diago assured the students, "I'm not expecting you to reach that standard straightaway. The routine I'm going to teach you is much simpler … for now."

Bella felt very excited as they warmed up. Rock 'n' roll dancing looked really cool! "I *so* want to do this," she whispered to Sofia and Natalie as they did their stretches. "Wouldn't it be amazing to dance in a West End musical?"

"Too awesome for words," Sofia agreed.

"And those costumes!" Natalie sighed. "I loved her dress. Rock 'n' roll rocks!"

Once everyone had warmed up, Mr Diago asked them to get into pairs. Bella went over to Jason who was her usual partner in dance classes. "Ready to have me throwing you around, Bee?" he asked with a wink.

Bella smiled back, liking her new nickname. "As long as you promise not to drop me," she giggled.

"We'll start with the basic six-step," Mr Diago announced. "Boys, you're dancing two steps to the left, two steps to the right, and then the rockback step, like so. Girls, you're mirroring the boys, so it's right, then left, then the rockback step on your right. Let's try it."

Mr Diago and Miss Anna showed them the basics and everyone copied. Then they added in some kicks, and some ball-change steps, gradually making the routine more complex and challenging.

Bella was enjoying herself. Back at the first audition, her dad had advised her to "dance like nobody's watching" – just for the sure joy of it – and it was advice she'd tried to follow ever since. She loved the feeling of dancing, the rhythm taking over her body. It always made her feel happy.

It was all too soon before Mr Diago stopped the music. "That's enough for today," he said. "I'll be running some more rock 'n' roll lessons before I choose the couples for the show. Thank you everyone – you did very well for a first time."

"You may now leave for a break before your jazz class," Miss Anna said. "Make sure you have a drink and something light to eat."

Hot and exhilarated, Bella was just about to leave the studio with her friends when Mr Diago called over to her. "You

– with the ponytail. Could you and your partner stay behind, please?"

Bella blinked. Mr Diago was looking right at her. "Me?" she said excitedly. *Oh my goodness,* she thought. *Was he going to tell them that he wanted her and Jason to be one of the couples for the show?*

Mr Diago nodded. "Yes, you," he said.
He wasn't smiling, Bella noticed with
a lurch, and her wonderful daydream
about being picked for the performance
vanished in the next second. "I think
we need a little more practice," he said.
"Can we take it from the top? Just you
on your own first, dear."

Bella's heart sank. Oh no. He thought
she needed more practice? Those were

*not* the words she'd hoped to hear. She swallowed. "Sure," she said. Maybe her lucky earrings hadn't been quite so lucky after all.

Bella began to dance solo for Mr Diago, hoping to impress him, but she couldn't help noticing how much he kept frowning. "Point your toes," he said, pausing the music and demonstrating. "Like this – see?"

Bella began again, trying to keep her toes perfectly pointed. "Your kicks should be higher," Mr Diago said this time. "Loosen up a bit, too. You've gone all stiff."

Bella gritted her teeth. *It's no wonder I look stiff, with you criticising me all the time,* she felt like saying. *Anyone would be stiff!*

Finally, Mr Diago asked Bella and Jason to dance together and watched them closely. By now, Bella had lost all her confidence and kept making mistakes.

"Don't worry about it," Jason whispered after she'd got the steps wrong again. "Forget he's watching. Just imagine it's me and you, dancing for fun."

The words were exactly what she needed to hear. Fun – yes, that's what was missing. She'd loved dancing rock 'n' roll style before Mr Diago started picking up all her faults. She had to try to enjoy herself.

Mr Diago asked them to go through the routine several times more and soon Bella was very tired and out of breath. She kept thinking about her friends having a cool drink and something to eat, and that only made her feel hotter and thirstier. Yet still Mr Diago didn't seem happy with her dancing. Every time they went through the routine, he'd find something else to criticise: the way she was holding her head, that her hips weren't swivelling enough, how her kicks should be more "rhythmical" ... Bella felt close to giving up. Just as she was on the verge of bursting into tears and running out of the room, Mr Diago turned the music off and nodded.

"Better," he said. "But you'll have to work hard over the next week. Thank you, you may both go now."

He left the room and Bella hung her head. "That was horrible," she said miserably.

Jason looked exhausted too. "He knows what he wants, doesn't he?" he said as he pulled on his hoodie.

"Yes, and I don't think it's me," Bella replied, stretching out her aching muscles in some cool-down exercises. She sighed. "To think I was excited about auditioning for his musical. Now I just feel totally fed up."

"I know what you mean," Jason said. "Oh well. You can't win them all, as my dad says. And we did just get a private masterclass from Manuel Diago – that's pretty amazing! Come on, let's go and see if there are any flapjacks left in the dining hall. I'm starving."

Bella dragged her tired feet as she followed him out of the studio. Jason was right, she reminded herself. She couldn't expect to shine at everything.

And she should think herself lucky to have had an extra session with such a talented, famous professional.

All the same, it had been pretty dispiriting, slogging through the routine again and again, just the two of them – like having a load of extra-hard homework dumped on you when your brain was already aching.

As she walked out into the corridor, she almost collided with Natalie, who was charging along at top speed. "Sorry!" Natalie called over her shoulder. "Just going to squeeze in some extra practice before the next class."

Bella opened her mouth to reply but Natalie had already vanished into a studio. Whew, she thought as she made her way towards the dining hall and a well-earned drink. Competition at the Strictly Dance Academy was definitely tough … and the pressure seemed to be hotting up all the time.

That night, Veronica was in a bad mood as the girls got ready for bed. She tutted when Natalie banged the door on her way out to practise again. She pulled a face when Sofia read aloud a funny section of her book. And she rolled her eyes whenever Bella said anything at all.

After a while, Bella couldn't stand it any longer. "Is something wrong, Veronica?" she asked politely.

Veronica gave her a withering look. "Why should anything be *wrong*? Why would I care about a nobody like you having extra time with Mr Diago?" She threw herself down on her bed and turned away. "It's so unfair," she said bitterly.

"Oh, Veronica, it really wasn't like that," Bella began. Honestly! If the other girl only *knew* how miserable it had been, she wouldn't be feeling remotely jealous. "It— "

"I'm not interested," Veronica snapped, pulling up the duvet around her ears. "I'm trying to sleep."

Sofia was frowning up at the clock.

"Where's Natalie?" she said. "It's lights out soon."

As if she'd heard the question, Natalie burst into the room in the very next moment. "Phew!" she sighed, kicking off her dance shoes and collapsing on to her bed. "I'm totally beat."

"I'm not surprised," Bella said. "Have

you seriously been dancing all this time? You are hardcore." Natalie was red in the face and her hair was damp with sweat. "You did eat something, didn't you?" Bella added, trying to remember whether she'd seen Natalie at dinner earlier.

"Sure, I grabbed a sandwich," Natalie said, not meeting her in the eye. She lay still for a moment, looking as if she'd used up every last shred of energy. "I suppose I'd better take a shower and go to bed … when I can be bothered to move again, that is."

Bella watched her friend stumble wearily to the bathroom and felt concerned. "She's working really hard," she commented to the others.

"Maybe even too hard. Don't you think?"

Veronica gave a scornful little laugh. "Some people need more practice than others," she sneered.

"Everyone needs to work hard," Sofia corrected her. "Let's keep an eye on Natalie," she added to Bella in a lower voice. "It's good to practise, but even the best dancers need some downtime too."

4

The following day, Mr Diago coached
the students in another session of
rock 'n' roll dancing. Frustratingly,
he seemed to spend most of the time
focused on Bella again, correcting her
and making her repeat each exercise
until she'd got them all perfect.

Veronica had cheered up hugely
now that she'd realised why Mr Diago
was spending so much time with Bella.

"Some people *do* seem to struggle with the simplest things," she heard Veronica say to another girl in a too-loud whisper.

Bella felt her cheeks turn red. It was embarrassing enough being singled out for needing extra help – but it was even worse having Veronica tittering and making mean remarks in the background.

Afterwards, she felt thoroughly crushed. "I might as well give up on the idea of this stupid gala performance," she grumbled to Sofia as they left the studio for their afternoon break. "Mr Diago obviously thinks I'm not good enough. What's the point of trying any more?"

"You *are* good enough," Sofia said

soothingly. "Don't give up now. You know what they say, practice makes perfect."

Bella didn't reply. She was starting to think that Mr Diago's ideas of perfection were out of her reach.

The girls were just queuing for drinks and buttered toast in the canteen when they heard excited whispering and giggling from the other students. Bella turned and saw Velma and Matt, the rock 'n' roll dancers who'd performed for them the day before, had joined the queue. Instantly she nudged Sofia, feeling thrilled to be so close to real professional dancers!

Sofia's eyes widened. "Cool!" she said, then grinned. "Hey, do you dare me to ask them for their autographs?"

Bella smiled. "I totally dare you," she replied. "Great idea." She glanced around. "Where's Natalie? I bet she'd love to meet them too."

But Natalie was nowhere to be seen. "I think she said something about going up to the dorm," Sofia replied. "She'll be gutted to have missed them. Come on!"

Giddy with excitement, Bella and Sofia hurried over to the dancers. "Hi," Sofia said politely. "I loved the dance you did for us yesterday. We're

the class who are being coached by Mr Diago."

"Oh hi," said Velma with a big smile. "How's it going? Are you enjoying rock 'n' rolling?"

"Rock 'n' rolling is brilliant," Bella said smiling back. "Hard work though."

"It is," Matt agreed. "Especially with a teacher like Manuel, right?"

Sofia and Bella exchanged a glance and laughed. "Right," Sofia replied. "Um … could we get your autographs, please?"

"Sure, sweetie," Velma said. She rummaged in her handbag and pulled out two old theatre tickets. "Shall I sign these? I don't have any paper."

"Yes, please," Bella breathed unable to

believe her luck.

"So you
guys are
hoping
to join
the gala
performance
next week,
huh?" Matt
said and

winked. "You know there are going to
be some really famous guests in the
audience that night, right?"

"Really?" Sofia said at once. "Like
who?"

Matt tapped his nose. "I couldn't
possibly say," he teased, signing the
tickets with a flourish. "You'll just have

to be picked to take part – then you'll see
for yourself!"

*

Meeting the professional dancers was
just the boost Bella needed to lift her out
of the glums. Even better was the news
that there might be a celebrity or two
watching the gala performance! Nobody
could talk about anything else for the
rest of breaktime. It was so exciting!

Their next lesson was ballroom
dancing, and Bella felt much more
cheerful as she went along to the studio
with the rest of the class. It wasn't until
Miss Frances, their teacher, came in that
she realised Natalie was still missing.
Strange!

"Let's pick up from where we left

off last week with the foxtrot," Miss Frances said, casting an eye around the room. She was tall and slender with high cheekbones and white-blonde hair. She was also extremely strict, and the sort of teacher who noticed *everything*.

Uh-oh, thought Bella, wondering where on earth her friend was.

Everyone went to stand with their partners. Bella was with Jason of course, but Natalie's usual dance partner, Leo, gazed around blankly. "Um … Miss Frances? My partner isn't here," he said.

"Not here? Is she ill?" Miss Frances replied.

There was silence for a moment. Leo looked over to Bella and Sofia for help, but they shrugged, not certain what to say. "We ... we haven't seen her since the last lesson," Bella said. "I'm sure she's on her way though."

Miss Frances' eyes narrowed with displeasure. "In that case, Leo, I'd better step in as your partner for this dance," she said. "Until Natalie can bring herself to turn up, that is!"

The class began and still Natalie didn't appear. Then, a full ten minutes into the lesson, the door opened and in she hurried, her face scarlet.

"I'm *so* sorry, Miss Frances," she gasped.

"I completely lost track of time."

Miss Frances drew herself up to her full height and gave Natalie a cold look. "I expect all students to be prompt and punctual," she snapped. "Do you want to learn from me, or not?"

"Yes, of course," Natalie said quickly, turning redder than ever, "but—"

"Then see to it that you arrive *punctually* for your lessons in future," the teacher said. "Otherwise you are not only letting your teachers down, you are letting *yourself* down. Make sure this doesn't happen again."

"Yes, Miss," Natalie said, her voice so low it was almost a whisper. "Sorry," she added.

Bella tried to catch Natalie's eye so

that she could give her a reassuring smile but the American girl seemed lost in thought as she crossed the studio to Leo. *Poor Natalie*, Bella thought sympathetically, seeing her friend's shoulders slumping. *She hasn't been acting herself lately. Is she all right?*

5

Natalie kept to herself during the class but Bella noticed that she wasn't dancing with her usual flair. Instead she moved mechanically around the studio with Leo as if her heart wasn't really in it.

As soon as practice was over, Natalie pulled on her hooded top and dashed out of the studio alone. Bella and Sofia went after her. "Hey!" Bella called, rushing down the corridor to catch up. "Are you OK? What happened earlier?"

"Where were you?" Sofia asked in the next breath.

Natalie gave them a little smile that didn't quite make it all the way up to her eyes. "I was so tired after our rock 'n' roll class that I went up to the dorm to lie down," she confessed. "I only meant to shut my eyes for a minute, but I must have fallen asleep." She sighed. "I don't think I'm Miss Frances' number one student now."

Bella linked an arm through hers. "I'm not surprised you're tired with all your extra practice," she said. "But you're definitely number one when it comes to effort. Anyway, listen, guess what we—"

She was about to tell her friend about the celebrity audience at the gala performance but Natalie interrupted, looking defensive. "I'm just enjoying being able to dance so much, that's all," she said stiffly. "Nothing wrong with that, is there?"

"No, of course, not," Bella said, wondering why Natalie was being so prickly. "I didn't mean—"

"Hey, I've just had the most brilliant idea," Sofia said as Bella floundered for the right words. "I know exactly what we need to cheer us up after all the teacher trauma today – a party in the dorm tonight!"

"Definitely," Bella said happily. "And a midnight feast!"

Even Natalie smiled. "Sofia, you're a genius," she said. "Count me in!"

*

After lights out that evening, Bella, Sofia and Natalie switched on their torches, crept out of bed and gathered up the snacks they had in their cupboards – crisps, sweets and half a packet of chocolate biscuits.

"What *are* you doing?" Veronica asked, sitting up in bed and pushing her turquoise velvet eye mask on top of her head.

"We're having a party," Sofia

replied with a grin. "Want to join us?"

Veronica thought about it. "Well, I might as well," she said in the end. "I won't be able to sleep if you're all mucking about."

"Cool," Sofia said, ignoring the rude tone of her reply. "Let's start with a midnight feast, then we can dance and play games. This will be the best dorm party that the Strictly Dance Academy has ever seen!"

The girls spread out the food, then Sofia put on some music at a low volume and they tucked in to their feast. They all discussed who might be coming to see the gala performance and were soon in fits of laughter, imagining the royal family, soap stars and all their favourite pop singers watching them dance on stage.

Then Sofia jumped up as a new song started. "Come on, guys," she said. "I love this one. Let's dance!"

Bella never needed to be persuaded to dance and leaped up as well. They moved the snacks out of trampling distance, and danced together, waving their torches above their heads like disco lights.

Smiling and laughing, Bella felt as if she was dancing all her cares away as she and the others made up funny routines to the music and took it in turns to lead. She'd never seen Veronica smile so much either – it made her face ten times prettier. As for Natalie … well, even she seemed to be enjoying herself and looking less shattered.

After a few songs, the girls took their
pillows off the beds and used them as
floor cushions to
sit on.

That was when Veronica went and spoiled everything.

"So," she said, propping herself up on an elbow and stretching her top leg up towards the ceiling, "what happened to you this afternoon, Natalie? How come you were so late for ballroom class? Not *more* extra practice sessions?"

Natalie flushed, and the sparkle vanished from her eyes. "No," she said, the same defensive note as earlier creeping back into her voice.

"I've met people like you before," Veronica went on airily. "There was a girl just the same at my last boarding school. For ever cramming, doing extra homework, swotting like crazy to impress the teachers. Went bonkers in the end and had to leave the school."

"Well I'm not like that," Natalie retorted. "For one thing I'm not crazy. For another, I'm not planning to leave the school. So just keep your nose out of my business, OK?"

Veronica held up her hands. "Touchy," she murmured, a smirk playing on her lips.

"There's nothing wrong with a bit of hard work," Bella put in, trying to make the peace.

"Who said there was? And so what if I'm working hard?" Natalie said sharply. "We're *supposed* to be working hard! And—"

Just as she was getting into full flow, the door opened suddenly, making them

all jump. "Girls!"
came a voice, and
there was Emma in
the doorway, a hand
on her hip. "What
are you doing?
You're meant to be
in bed, asleep!"

The four girls
scrambled for
their beds and
lay down in them
immediately.

"Sorry, Emma," Sofia said meekly.

"Go to sleep now," she replied. "And
no more noise. I could hear you all the
way down the corridor!"

She closed the door again and Bella

waited until she heard Emma's footsteps padding away. Then she sat up in bed and leaned over towards Natalie. "Sorry if I annoyed you," she whispered. "I didn't mean to."

Natalie was turned away from the others, facing the wall, and for a horrible moment, Bella thought she was going to ignore the apology. But then she heard a whispered reply. "It's OK."

Bella wriggled into a more comfortable position and tried to doze off but Natalie's words rang around her head. *It's OK,* she'd said – but it was clear as crystal that things were really *not* OK for Natalie. Bella had to find out what was going on in her friend's head ... and hopefully find a way to help.

The next afternoon, when Bella's class walked into the studio for their dance lesson, they saw that Mr Diago was already there waiting for them.

"Good afternoon, everyone," he said. "Today will be your final practice session with me before tomorrow's audition so I expect you all to try your very hardest to perfect the routine while you can. Let's warm up first, then I want to see your best dancing. Off we go!"

Full of determination to impress Mr Diago – just for once! – Bella poured everything she had into the routine, and tried to remember all the pointers he'd given her.

But as usual, her best just wasn't
enough for the perfectionist teacher.
Moments later, he was at her side,
correcting her on the position of her feet,
and the height of her kicks. If it hadn't
been for Jason's encouragement and the
keep-going looks Sofia and Natalie
were sending her, Bella would
have thrown her hands in the air
with frustration and given up there
and then.

At the end of the session, Mr Diago
had a nice surprise at least. "Well done,
all of you," he said. "There's only one
thing you need to do now and that's
get fitted out with some costumes for
tomorrow's audition!"

Bella cheered up immediately. Yay!

The costume room was like an Aladdin's cave of wonderful outfits in every kind of fabric, as well as accessories and shoes galore. Going there always felt like the most fun kind of shopping trip – and best of all, you didn't have to pay for anything!

Sofia looked pleased too, although Natalie's face fell. "Oh," she said. "Does that mean we don't have any more dance classes today?"

Mr Diago nodded. "That's right," he said. "You have the rest of the afternoon off, once you've chosen your costume. Use the time to relax, if possible. You've all earned a break."

Natalie didn't look too keen on taking a break, Bella thought as the three friends went along to the costume room together. In fact, she kept casting longing looks at the practice studios they passed, as if she'd much rather be dancing.

"This is a waste of time," Natalie grumbled. "Only three couples are going to be picked, aren't they? Why bother fitting everyone out in a costume when most of us will only wear them for one audition?"

"I think it'll be fun to audition in full costume," Bella said and giggled. "Do you think they'll gel our hair into quiffs and rocker styles as well?"

Sofia laughed but Natalie didn't even smile. Bella couldn't help an anxious glance at her as they reached the costume room. What was making

Natalie so uptight? She seemed a
million miles from the fun-loving girl
Bella had first met.

"Hey guys and dolls," said Harriet
when Bella's class walked into the
costume room. She and a man called
Richard were in charge of the costumes
and were both really friendly. "So ...
you're all going to be rock 'n' rollers, are
you? Let's see what we can find."

Bella's eye was caught by a blue top
with silver sequins and a matching white
skirt with blue spots. The skirt was short
and full with lots of netting underneath
that peeped out of the bottom. Sofia
examined a white sleeveless dress
which had red polka dots all over the
skirt. Veronica made a beeline for a

pink skirt and top with gold finishing,
while the boys skimmed through the
sparkly jackets hanging on a rail. The
only person who wasn't enthusiastically
hunting for their perfect costume
was Natalie.

"Which colour are you going for, Natalie?" Bella called out encouragingly. "I think green really suits you."

Natalie shrugged. "Oh, anything," she said, glancing at her watch. "I guess if I just pick any old thing, I can slope away and ..."

Harriet had overheard and looked shocked. "If you 'just pick any old thing'?" she repeated back to Natalie sternly. "I don't think so! In fact, I'm going to help you find the perfect and most gorgeous costume myself now, so there." She cocked her head on one side thoughtfully. "Let's try you in something silver," she said after a moment. "Bear with me."

Natalie rolled her eyes as if she

couldn't care less, then checked her
watch again. Clearly she was dying to
get away and practise some more … but
why?

"Maybe after this we could go for a
swim or something," Bella suggested.
"Or see if the ping-pong table's free?"

Natalie wrinkled her nose. "Nah," she
said.

Bella sighed. "Natalie … You don't
have to keep practising all the time,"
she said, choosing her words carefully
so that her friend wouldn't blow her top
again. "You're naturally really good.
And you heard what Mr Diago said – we
should all chill out this afternoon. If you
keep practising, you'll—"

"Look, Bella," Natalie interrupted,

sounding irritated. "I know you're trying to be kind but please do me a favour and just butt out. I'm fine, OK? I'm absolutely FINE!"

She practically shouted the last word, and Harriet, who was just coming over with a silver sequined dress over one arm, stopped and stared in surprise. "Perhaps we should go for a little chat," she said calmly. "Come on, both of you. Into my private dressing room. Let's sort this out between us." Bella was relieved that Harriet had taken charge of the situation but

Natalie looked distinctly unhappy about the prospect of "a little chat". Both girls followed Harriet through a door marked "Private" and found themselves in a small dressing area complete with a full-length mirror and vanity table. There were two folding chairs against the wall, and Harriet motioned for the girls to set them up and sit down while she pulled out the swivel stool that was tucked under the vanity table.

"Now then," she said, wheeling around to face them. "What's going on, Natalie? Where's that cheerful beaming smile of yours gone, hmm?"

"I'm just a bit tired," Natalie replied, folding her arms across her chest and not looking at either Bella or Harriet.

"She's been doing lots of extra practice," Bella said tentatively, and swallowed. She really didn't want to antagonise Natalie but it needed to be said. "We're worried she's overdoing it a bit. Sorry, Nat!" she said, as her roommate glared at her. "But it's true. I'm your friend – I want you to be happy. But lately I don't think you have been."

Natalie sighed and scuffed her feet along the floor. There was a long silence. "I guess ..." she began, then broke off and sighed again.

"Go on," Harriet said encouragingly.

"I guess I'm just feeling kinda ... worried," she said in a small voice.

"About what?" Bella asked. She

reached out and squeezed Natalie's hand.

Natalie hesitated but then said, "You know at the auditions to get into the academy, how you and Sofia got straight through and I didn't?"

Bella nodded. It had been awful when Natalie hadn't been given a place at first – she'd run out of the audition studio crying with disappointment. Bella had felt so sorry for her she'd even offered

Natalie *her* place. "But Miss Anna changed her mind," Bella reminded her. "She decided you should stay after all – and I'm so glad she did."

Natalie gave a small smile. "Me too," she replied. "But I can't help feeling that she might change her mind back at any moment. What if she decides that she was right first time and I shouldn't be here?" She hung her head. "That's why I want to keep practising. I have to prove that she was right to give me a chance."

"Oh, Natalie," Harriet said. "I'm sorry to hear you've been worrying. But working yourself into exhaustion is not the answer. Tell me, since you started at the academy, has Miss Anna ever shown any signs of regret to have picked you?"

"No way," Bella said before Natalie could reply. "In fact, Natalie was chosen to dance with New Ride just last month. *And* I saw Miss Anna praising her in our jazz lesson on Monday."

Harriet smiled. "It doesn't sound to me as if she made the wrong decision to give you a place here, then," she said gently. "Not at all. Listen, I'd better go out and help the others with their costumes but, Natalie, I don't think you have anything to worry about. Be a little kinder to yourself. You're doing very well from what Bella says."

She left the girls on their own and Natalie took a deep breath. "Thank you," she said quietly. "I feel as if I've been going nuts lately, stressing out so much."

"I know what you mean," Bella said, still holding her hands. "I feel under pressure too from Mr Diago bossing me about all the time. Maybe we both need to go a bit easier on ourselves."

Natalie nodded. "You're right," she said, then leaned over and gave Bella a hug. "Thanks for being my friend." Then she picked up the silver dress Harriet had chosen for her. "I'd better try this on then, right? And after that, I'm going to take you up on that ping-pong idea. Prepare to be thrashed!"

Bella grinned. "Sounds like a plan to me," she replied. "Only I'd better warn you – you are so *not* going to thrash me. Got that?"

7

The following day, there was a jittery
atmosphere in the run-up to the
audition. Veronica in particular seemed
desperate to get a place in the gala
performance, and she and some of
the other girls couldn't stop chatting
anxiously about how they hoped they'd
be picked.

Bella, on the other hand, felt quite
detached. She was so sure that she

wouldn't be chosen that she didn't feel
at all nervous, or even very excited. She
was just glad that this was the last time
she'd have to dance in front of Mr Diago
and face his criticism.

The pupils were told to change into
their audition costumes and meet in
the reception area of the main building.
"You won't be auditioning here in the
practice studio," Miss Anna informed
them. "You will be driven to the theatre
in the West End to audition on stage
instead!"

Squeals and gasps greeted her
announcement, and even Bella began to
feel more enthusiastic. Wow! Dancing
on a West End stage ... now that was
cool. Then something even better

happened. Miss Anna beckoned for Natalie to come over, and put an arm around her. "I hear you have been worrying, yes?" she asked, then shook her head and made a tutting noise. "You do not need to worry," she said firmly. "Definitely not. You are a good dancer, Natalie. I am glad you are here. But too much worrying and too much work is not good, OK? So, how do you say in English? You must chill off."

Natalie chuckled. "I think you mean 'chill out', Miss Anna," she said, looking much happier. "And thank you. I'll try."

"Good. Excellent," Miss Anna said warmly. "So now … To the coach!"

\*

When they arrived at the theatre, everyone was more excited than ever. Bella felt as if her tummy was turning somersaults as they walked backstage, and she touched her lucky sparkly heart earrings. If ever she needed extra luck, it was today!

The students had their hair and make-up done by the theatre team which was

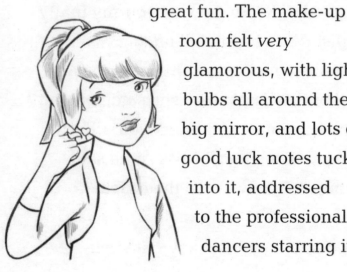

great fun. The make-up room felt *very* glamorous, with light bulbs all around the big mirror, and lots of good luck notes tucked into it, addressed to the professional dancers starring in

the musical night
after night.
Several large
posters were
on the walls,
advertising
stage
productions
gone by, some
featuring really
famous actors
and dancers. Bella wished with all her
heart that one day she might be lucky
enough to dance in a real West End
show herself.

"I love it here," she sighed to Sofia,
as they watched Natalie have her hair
pulled into a high swingy ponytail. "The

whole place has such a great feeling."

"I know," Sofia agreed. "I hope my feet behave themselves when I audition. I want to dance in the show more than ever now."

A lady called Evie was styling Bella's hair. She swept it up into a high ponytail and tied it back with a blue sparkly ribbon that matched her top. "Now you're ready to rock 'n' roll," said Evie with a smile.

"I sure am," Bella replied, smiling back. She glanced at her reflection and could hardly believe that the girl in the amazing outfit was truly her. "Wow," she said quietly. "I look like a real dancer now."

Sofia gave her a nudge. "For the fifty millionth time, Bella Jones, you *are* a

real dancer," she laughed. "Come on.
We've got to meet Miss Anna and Mr
Diago on stage now.
This is it!"

Bella felt more
and more
excited
as she
walked
back
through
the theatre
and on to
the stage
with the rest
of the
students.

Seeing all her friends dressed up so colourfully made everything seem rather dream-like and unreal. *This is it,* she heard Sofia say again in her head and a shiver went down her spine.

"Good afternoon, everyone," said Mr Diago. "Time to show me what you can do! As you might have heard, there will be some celebrity guests at our gala performance next week – including some of the professionals and celebrities on Strictly Come Dancing! So I'm looking for the very best dancers."

A buzz of thrilled whispers went rushing around the room at this news but Bella's high spirits had plummeted. The very best dancers? She knew that wasn't her, however much she wished she could take part. After Mr Diago had been so critical all week, she didn't stand a chance. *I'll just dance at the back of the stage and get this over with,* she thought to herself. *Hopefully if I'm there, he won't be able to see me – and he might leave me alone for once!*

Mr Diago clapped his hands and asked them to stand with their partners and spread out around the stage so that everyone had enough room to dance. Bella grabbed Jason and headed for the back behind Natalie and Leo where they'd be out of sight. "This looks like a good spot," she said.

Jason looked puzzled. "If you say so," he replied. "We'd stand a better chance of being noticed if we were closer to the audience though."

Bella shook her head. "I've had enough of being noticed this week, thanks," she told him.

Mr Diago, however, had other thoughts. "Bella and Jason – don't skulk all the way over there," he called. "Come out and dance in the front here. You, dear, in the pink – Victoria, is it? – could you move back to let Bella and Jason in, please."

Oh dear. Veronica looked furious at being moved *and* being called by the wrong name. "Sorry," Bella mouthed as she and Jason came to the front.

"That's better," Mr Diago said. "Right then – is everyone ready to dazzle me with your dancing one last time? This is the big one, people – make it count!"

Bella felt more jittery than ever as Mr Diago and Miss Anna went to sit in the audience seats. Jason gripped her hand. "You'll be brilliant, Bee," he told her.

Bella smiled at him, thinking for the hundredth time how glad she was to have Jason as her dance partner. "So will you," she replied.

The music began and off they went. *Dance like nobody's watching*, Bella reminded herself. *Do it because you love it!*

And she *did* love it, she thought, spinning lightly away from Jason, holding hands, and then letting him reel her back to him. Nothing else in the world made her feel as happy as when she was dancing. And just look at her now – in full costume and make-up on a West End stage. *I'll never forget this,* she thought joyfully. *Never in a million years!*

But her joyful feeling didn't last long.

"Stop the music!" Mr Diago shouted suddenly and came on to the stage. "Bella, with that last move, you seemed to forget to—"

It was the last straw. Bella just couldn't bear it any more.

Before she could stop herself, Bella ran off into the wings, tears pouring down her hot face. She didn't have a clue where she was going – all she knew was that she had to get away.

**8**

*Well, I've really gone and blown it now,* Bella thought moments later. She was lost backstage, having blundered blindly along the corridor, and felt absolutely awful. What had she *done*? Storming off-stage in front of Mr Diago and Miss Anna ... How unprofessional could you get?

To think it was Natalie who'd worried Miss Anna might change her mind about her being at the academy! Their teacher was probably phoning Bella's parents right now, telling them that their daughter was unteachable and needed to toughen up and deal with criticism more maturely. She'd ruined everything!

"Bella! Wait!" came a voice, and Bella turned to see Sofia hurrying towards her, with Miss Anna close behind. What an idiot they must think she was!

Bella wiped the tears away. "I'm sorry," she blurted out miserably, "but I just couldn't stand it." She put her head in her hands, wishing for the first time since she'd started at the academy that she could be back home with her mum and dad, and all her old friends. "I'm sorry," she whispered again.

"Oh Bella," Sofia said, hugging her. "Don't cry. Come back and try again."

Bella shook her head. "I can't," she said. "I'm just not good enough for Mr Diago."

There came footsteps along the corridor, and then a voice. "There you are! Whatever's wrong?"

Oh no. It was Mr Diago. Bella felt hotter and more embarrassed than ever. She sniffed and wiped her eyes. "I'm sorry I ran away," she said woodenly, her lip trembling. "I just …"

"You'd just had it up to here with me

criticising your steps," he finished, and patted her gently on the shoulder. "I don't blame you, Bella. All my dancers say the same thing. I know I'm a hard taskmaster."

"I'm sorry I'm not up to standard," Bella said humbly. "I've tried my absolute best, I promise, but I haven't had any dance lessons before, so I know I'm a bit behind the others." Her hands were shaking and she hid them behind her back so nobody would notice.

"Bella – that's the thing," Mr Diago said. "You *are* up to standard. In fact, your dancing is *above* standard. You have so much raw talent – you're a natural. Don't look so surprised. I noticed you straightaway, during that

very first lesson – you absolutely shone.
And that's why I've been so tough on
you – because I believe you can be even
better. I'm just trying to help."

Miss Anna put an arm around Bella.
"I think he forgets you are still only
nine years old," she said. "He is used to
telling off the big grown-up dancers –
not young girls. He has been a little hard
on you, perhaps."

"I'm sorry, Bella," Mr Diago said.
"Miss Anna's right – I've treated you
like one of my professionals. But believe
me, if I thought you were below standard
in any way, I wouldn't have spent so
much time with you. I only do that with
people I think can be real stars."

Bella gulped. She could hardly

believe what she was hearing. Mr Diago thought she was a natural. He thought she might become a real star! *Mamma mia*, as Sofia would say.

"Wow," she said, blinking as she tried to take all of this in.

Sofia grabbed her hand and squeezed it. "There – Bella! I said you were good, didn't I?" she said.

Mr Diago smiled. "She *is* good," he agreed. "So good in fact that I don't think you need to finish the rest of the audition, Bella. I want you and Jason to be the lead couple for the gala performance next week."

Bella squealed. "No way!" she cried.

"That's wonderful," said Miss Anna warmly, and Sofia gave a great cheer and hugged her. "You did it, Bella!"

Mr Diago was grinning broadly. "Why don't we go back to the stage and break the good news to Jason?" he suggested. "And then you can both relax while I choose the other two couples."

"Thank you," Bella managed to say through her smile. "Thank you for pushing me, and for letting me dance in your show. I promise I won't let you down."

"I know you won't," Mr Diago said. "Because I'll be watching you like a hawk during rehearsals, and I'll make sure you're ready."

"Thank you too, Sofia," Bella said as they went back towards the stage. She felt as if she might float along, she was so full of fizzy happiness. "Thanks for persuading me to keep trying. I'm glad I didn't give up."

"I'm glad too," Sofia said. "Now, I'd better find my partner and finish this audition. Wish me luck, Bella. I want to join you in the show!"

Back on stage, Bella saw Mr Diago tell Jason the good news. With a whoop of excitement, he punched the air, before remembering his manners and thanking Mr Diago for the opportunity. Then he ran across to Bella and the two of them whirled around happily in the wings together.

"We did it, Bee! We're in the show!"

"I know! Best news ever!" Bella laughed. She couldn't stop smiling.

"Just think … me and you dancing on this very stage, in front of hundreds and hundreds of people in the West End – including the Strictly stars! I can't quite believe it, Jason."

"Me neither," Jason agreed. The music started up again and they watched as the students began their audition routine from the top.

Bella laughed as Jason took her hand and they danced the routine themselves, hidden away in the wings. They knew the steps so well after all their practice, and kicked and twirled like never before. "I'm so glad we're both at the Strictly Dance Academy," Jason said as he spun Bella around.

"Me too," Bella said. "It's the best thing that's ever happened to me – and with our performance coming up next, I think it's just going to get better and better!"

9

Bella had performed in front of an audience before, but dancing on a West End stage was a completely new experience. The entire day had already become one she knew she'd never forget – starting with the sleek chauffeur-driven car that picked up her and Jason from the Strictly Academy, through the glamorous hair and make-up process, to the fizzy, excited atmosphere backstage.

A bouquet of
sweet-smelling
flowers had
been delivered
to Bella's
dressing room, with a
note which read "Good
luck tonight, Bella! You'll
be wonderful! Love Miss
Anna, Sofia, Natalie and
all your friends at the academy." Just
reading the words had been enough to
give her goosebumps.

And now here she was, waiting in
the wings, butterflies flipping and
flapping in her tummy, aware that there
were over one thousand people in the
audience tonight. Thank goodness Jason

was beside her – calm, steady Jason. "Ready for this?" he asked.

Bella hesitated. She hadn't slept at all well the night before. Despite the countless hard hours of practice she'd put in with Mr Diago, she was still dreading making a silly mistake on stage in front of everyone – the audience, the celebrity dancers who were performing tonight, and Mr Diago himself of course. "I think so," she managed to say.

"You'll be great, Bee," Jason told her and squeezed her hand. "I know you will."

Bella's mouth dried up as she heard the beginning of the piece of music that they'd be dancing to. Any moment now it would be their cue!

"OK, guys," Mr Diago said, appearing beside them. "This is it. Enjoy your big moment!"

Before Bella could stutter a thank you in reply, she heard their cue and in the next moment, she and Jason were dancing out on stage together just as they'd rehearsed so many times. She blinked in the bright lights then felt a huge surge of energy as the crowd applauded their entrance – whoah! Adrenalin raced through her body and almost immediately, her nerves vanished. She could do this!

One, two, kick! Three, four, spin! Bella knew the routine backwards and she and Jason danced it perfectly while an enormous smile broke on her face. *I'm*

*really here, dancing on a West End stage,*
she kept thinking dazedly. *And it feels
incredible!*

The routine was over all too soon –
and so was the end of the evening's
performance. Bella beamed as the
audience gave
them the

most thunderous round of applause she had ever heard, and she, Jason and the rest of the dancers bowed once, twice, and three times!

Gazing out at the sea of faces before her, Bella felt tingles all over. There was Mr Diago clapping in the wings, looking almost tearful with pride. There, in the front row, was an actress from one of Bella's favourite soaps smiling right at her! And best of all, one of the celebrity dancers made a point of turning on stage

to applaud Bella and Jason, making
Bella blush with sheer happiness.

She would never forget this moment –
never in a million years. She was being
applauded on a West End stage! It had
turned out that dreams really did come
true after all.

See how Bella and her friends
learn to jive in

JUMPING
JIVE

*Read on for a sneak peek ...*

"Make sure you keep the beat, girls!"
Miss Anna clapped her hands in time to
the music as the Strictly Dance Academy
girls went through their routine for the
third time that afternoon. "One and two,
three and four," Miss Anna counted
out the steps of the complicated samba
section in the middle of the dance she'd
choreographed for them. Bella took a
breath and concentrated as hard as she

could on getting the
steps right. As they
came to the final few
moves of the routine, she
kicked her leg as high as
possible. Miss Anna was
always telling them to "kick
high to the sky!"

Bella raised her arms
for the finishing position
and broke out into an
enormous smile. Every day
at the academy she was
learning something
new and she totally
loved it!

"Excellent dancing
everrrryone!" Miss

Anna said, as the music stopped, "You are working as hard as my students back in Russia!"

Bella grinned over at Sofia and Natalie. She thought how happy she was she'd met them. Dancing was *always* Bella's favourite thing to do but it was even better when she was dancing right next to her best friends!

Sofia grinned back and Natalie winked – they were enjoying being in the academy every bit as much as Bella.

*I really am in the best school in the world*, Bella thought. Even after a couple of months, she still found it hard to believe that she really belonged. She remembered when she had come to the

auditions with her dad. She had been
one of the least experienced girls to try
for a place and yet she'd been picked to
be in the Strictly Dance Academy! Not
only that, but since Bella had started
training, she'd been chosen to dance in
a carnival with the band New Ride and
to perform in a gala performance of a
West-End musical. Sometimes it felt as if
she wasn't so much in a dancing school
as on a dancing roller coaster!

Miss Anna clapped her hands again
to get everyone's attention. "Now,
everyone, make sure you do your
stretching exercises properly – we *do not*
want any pulled muscles . . .'

Bella shuddered. She couldn't bear
the thought of not being able to dance

because of an injury. She was about
to start her stretching routine when
Miss Anna called over. "Bella, Natalie,
Sofia and Veronica, may I see you for a
moment?"

Bella ran over with the other three
girls, her heart thumping. That was the
thing about being in the Strictly Dance
Academy – you never knew what was
going to happen next!

Miss Anna waited for the rest of the
class to leave and then turned to the four
girls. "I have some news for you," she
said, smiling. "A film producer has been
in touch with the academy."

*A film producer!* Bella felt a buzz of
excitement run through her. *What was
this about?*

"He's looking for some junior dancers for a scene in his new film," Miss Anna went on. "But the problem is, he can't hold regular auditions because the whole project is top secret."

"Top secret?" Sofia asked.

"Yes. Because the star of the film is Jet Rogerson," Miss Anna said.

The three girls gasped. *Jet Rogerson!* Bella's insides did a triple twirl. Jet Rogerson was the most famous actor in the entire world! Not only that, he was also Bella's *favourite* actor in the entire world!

"The film is set during the 1950s and there's a scene set at a prom with a big dance number," Miss Anna continued. "So you'll all learn the routine and then one of you will be chosen to dance it with Jet."

Bella shook her head in shock. She could hardly believe it. She had a poster of Jet Rogerson up on the wall of their dorm and now she was going to get the chance to meet him . . . it was like a dream!

"Whoo-hoo!" Natalie's eyes were shining. "That is a-ma-zing!"

"A chance to be in a Jet Rogerson film?" Sofia said, bouncing on her toes, "as my mum would say, it's inc*rrrrr*redible!"

Bella laughed. She loved it when Sofia did impressions of her Italian p*rrrr*ima ballerina mother!

"It's seriously incredible," Bella said. She felt goosebumps at the back of her neck.

Even Veronica was impressed. "His movies aren't bad at all," she said. "And as I've had quite a bit of acting experience I'm sure being in a film will come naturally for me."

Natalie rolled her eyes and Bella couldn't help smiling. It wasn't the first time Veronica had acted like a diva and it probably wouldn't be the last!

The chance to dance with her favourite actor in the whole world! Bella couldn't imagine how life at the Strictly Dance Academy could get any more exciting. As the girls waited for Miss Anna to explain what would happen next, Bella kept picturing Jet Rogerson as he looked on her poster – with his dark blue eyes and his shock of jet-black hair. Was it really possible she was going to meet him in person? She had to force herself to stop daydreaming and listen to Miss Anna.

"I talked it over with the school principal, Mr Goodwin," Miss Anna told them. "We felt that the four of you are not only talented enough to be considered, but you have all been working extremely hard. That's why we chose you for these secret tryouts."

Bella shivered with excitement. Mr

Ben Goodwin thought she was good enough to audition for a movie starring Jet Rogerson! This really was her best day at the academy yet!

"Now," Miss Anna went on briskly. "There's no time to lose. Your first day on set is this afternoon. You'll be meeting the set choreographer and learning the dance today, and then tomorrow you'll have the audition."

"Tomorrow?" Bella felt her heart race. There was so little time to get ready!

Miss Anna smiled. "Don't worry, you'll all be fine."

"What kind of dance will we be doing?" Bella asked.

"A really fun one!" Miss Anna said. "The jive!"

"Ooh, that's one of my all-time favourites!" called a familiar voice.

Bella looked up to see Pam, the cleaning lady at the Strictly Dance Academy. She walked up with a pair of dusters in her hand.

"You'll have to be quick on your feet for the jive," Pam warned them, shaking a duster at Bella.

"That's true," Miss Anna agreed. "It's a very quick dance, and needs excellent foot work."

**Read
Jumping Jive
to find out what
happens next!**

*Meet the characters at the*
*Strictly Dance Academy*

## Character profile:

Natalie

★ Age: 9

★ Favourite colour: green

★ Favourite dance: rock 'n' roll because it reminds Natalie of home.

★ Favourite outfit: the dress Natalie wore to samba at the carnival in *Samba Sensation* because it had sparkling sequins that spelled out her name!

★ Favourite accessory: Natalie loves her jazz shoes as they are covered with silver glittery stars!

★ Favourite dance partner: Natalie is usually paired with Leo for ballroom dance classes and together they dance a fantastic foxtrot!

★ Natalie started dancing when she was five.

**Fun fact** *Natalie is American but has been living in England for two years after her dad got a job here. She'll never lose her accent though!*

# WIN AN IPOD SHUFFLE!

Read our Strictly Come Dancing books *Rock 'n' Rolling* and *Jumping Jive*, answer the questions below, and soon you could be practising your dance moves on the go with a fabulous iPod Shuffle!

## QUESTION 1

What is the name of the West End musical Bella auditions for in *Rock 'n' Rolling*?

a) Grease
b) Slick
c) Hairspray

## QUESTION 2

Which Hollywood star does Bella get to dance with in *Jumping Jive*?

a)   Jet Rogerson
b)   Jim Rocking
c)   Josh Robinson

## JUST SEND YOUR ANSWERS, WITH YOUR NAME AND ADDRESS, ON A POSTCARD TO:

Strictly Come Dancing iPod Shuffle Competition,
Marketing Department, Hodder Children's Books,
338 Euston Road, London, NW1 3BH.

### BY 31 JANUARY 2013

## Runner-up prizes are also available!

See full terms and conditions at www.hodderchildrens.co.uk

# Join our Review Crew and receive a free book!*

## Be the first to read great new books!

The Review Crew are a group of passionate readers who help us by reviewing new and upcoming books before they've even hit the shops!

Members of the Review Crew receive free copies of our books in manuscript form and tell us what they think by filling in a simple questionnaire. We also like to ask for feedback about cover designs.

**If you'd like to claim your free book and join the hundreds of other kids getting involved, just visit:**

## www.hachettechildrens.co.uk/reviewcrew

**and sign up today!**

Or, fill in the form overleaf and post to: Review Crew, Hachette Children's Books, 338 Euston Road, London, NW1 3BH

First Name (in BLOCK capitals)...................................................

Surname (in BLOCK capitals)....................................................

Are you ☐ Male or ☐ Female?

Date of Birth: DAY ☐☐ MONTH ☐☐ YEAR ☐☐☐☐

Email Address...................................................................

Address.........................................................................

.................................................................................

.................................................................................

Postcode.......................................

If you are under 12 years old please ask a parent/guardian to sign below – otherwise we won't be able to send you anything!

Parent/Guardian Signature.........................................................

Name (in BLOCK capitals)..........................................................

Date...............................................

As we can only send out a limited number of printed manuscripts, we would also like to be able to send you electronic versions of our books.

☐ Please tick this box if you either own or have access to an e-reader.